HARPER'S FLOWERS

SONYA COAXUM

Published by:

Little Oaks Publishing
18896 Greenwell Springs Road
Greenwell Springs, LA 70739
www.thepublishedword.com

ISBN: 978-1-940461-98-4 Trade Paper Version
ISBN: 978-1-950398-18-8 Case Laminate Version

Printed on demand in the U.S., the U.K. and Australia
For Worldwide Distribution

Dedication

This book is dedicated to my parents, who were educators.

Harper ran into the kitchen where her mom was cooking breakfast and hugged her mom with excitement.

"Good morning, Mom."

"Good morning, Harper. You are very happy this morning."

"Are we still going in the garden today to pick flowers?" asked Harper.

"Yes, Harper. After we eat breakfast, we will go to the garden."

Harper loves the smell of flowers in her
mother's garden.
She loves how beautiful the flowers look.

She ran around the garden, skipping and singing. There was one flower Harper always liked more than the others.

"Oh, Mom, the flowers are so beautiful! I especially love sunflowers! Can we pick a few sunflowers for me to put in a vase in my room?"

"Well, of course, Harper," said Mom.

As Harper was picking a few sunflowers, she saw something at the end of the plant that looked strange.

"Mom, what is this?"

"It is the root of the plant," said Mom. "Always remember, when you pick sunflowers, pull gently so you do not pull out the roots."

Harper looked at the flower closely with a strange look on her face and began to wonder why plants have roots.

"Mom, why do plants have roots?"

"Harper, please bring me the first flower you picked."

"Harper, plants are very beautiful, but they have parts just like your body has parts, like your legs, which help you walk, and hands, which help you hold things."

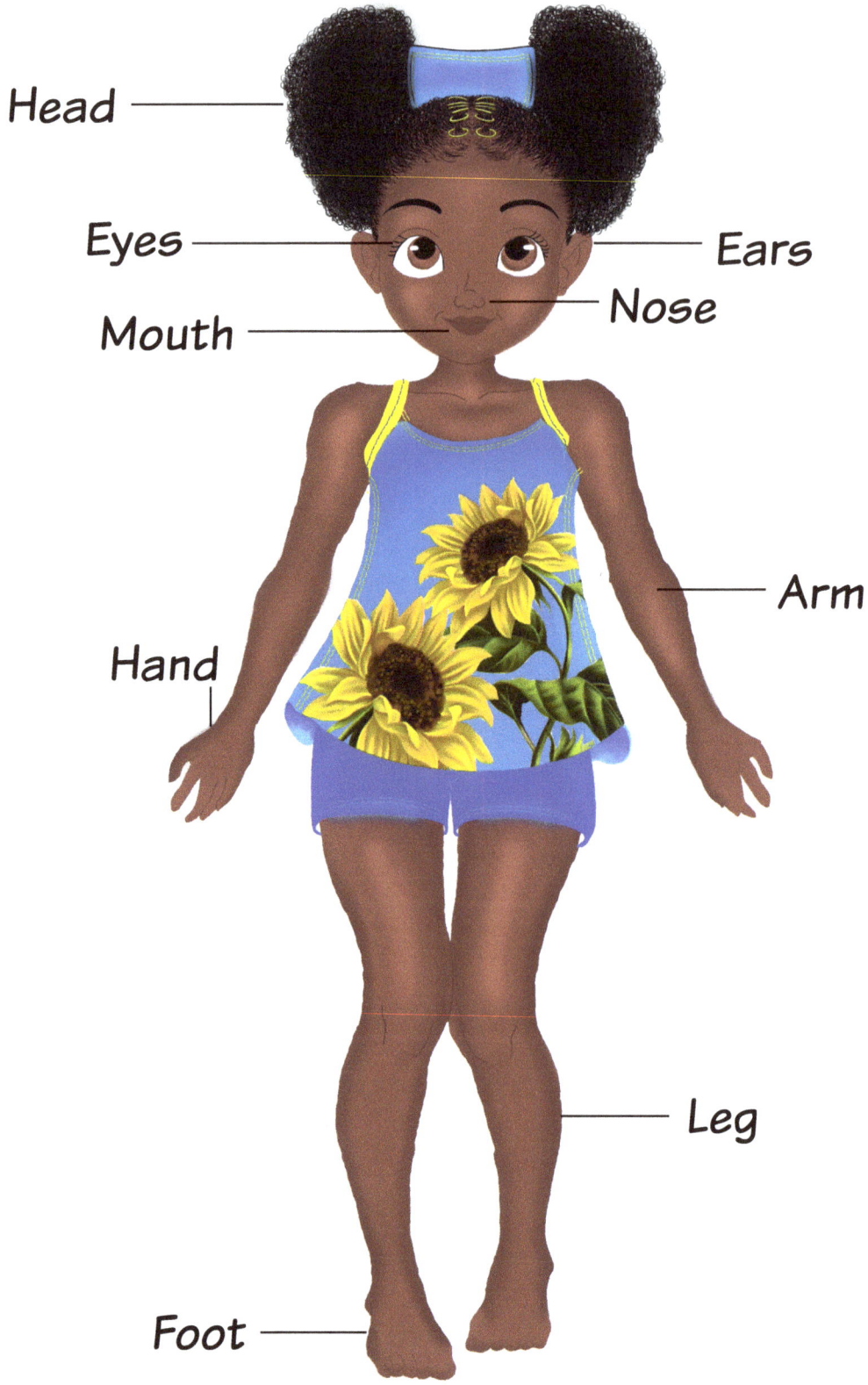

Head

Eyes

Mouth

Ears

Nose

Arm

Hand

Leg

Foot

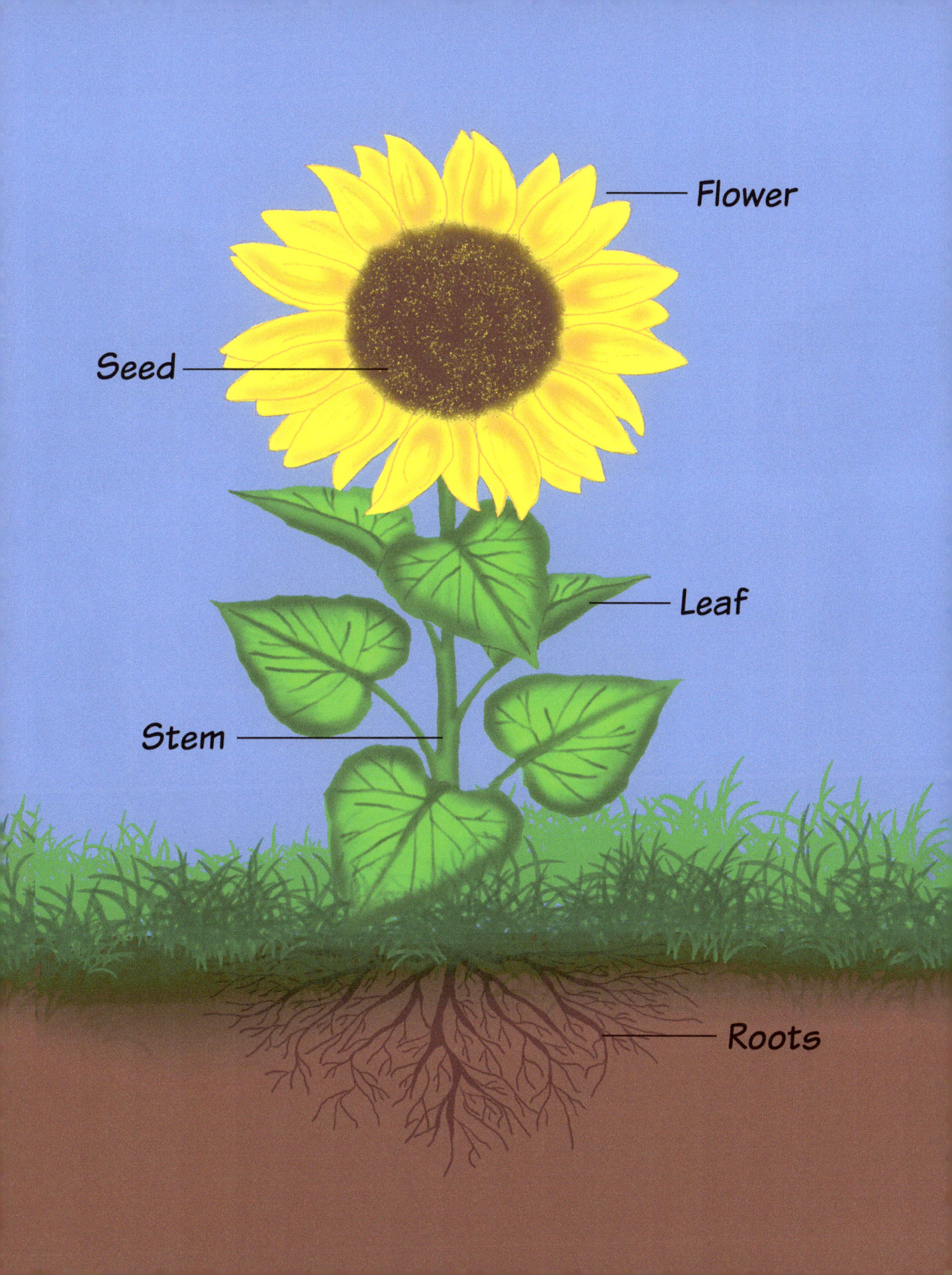

Flower

Seed

Leaf

Stem

Roots

"The long stringy parts of the plant are the roots. They hold the plants in the ground and provide nutrients and water from the soil," said Mom.

"Well, Mom, what is this long green piece?" asked Harper with bright, beaming eyes.

"Do you remember yesterday when I asked your brother to water the plants?"

"Yes, Mom."

"Well, Harper, the stem carries water and nutrients from the roots to other parts of the plant, which helps them to grow and look beautiful," said Harper's mom, smiling at her curious daughter.

"Harper, you know these are leaves of the flower. You probably did not know leaves make the oxygen you breathe, and they make food for the plant. The stem helps hold the plant upright to receive sunlight."

"Wow! I did not know leaves make food for plants," said Harper.

"Yes, it is called photosynthesis."

Harper tried to pronounce what her mother said. "Photo... What did you say?" asked Harper.

"I said 'photosynthesis,' which you will learn more about as you get older."

"Okay, Mom, but the prettiest part of the sunflower, to me, is the yellow petals."
"Yes, Harper, petals are the most beautiful part of the flower."

Harper looked at her mom with a curious look on her face.

"Mom, what is the dried part of the sunflower in the middle of the petals?

Sunflower Oil

"Those are the seeds of the sunflower. The seeds can be used for oil and in recipes for cooking," said Mom.

"Wow! Mom, I only like sunflowers because they are so pretty, but I did not know they could be used for cooking."

"Mom, I love how the beautiful sunflowers grow in your garden. Can we continue picking sunflowers now?"

"Yes, Harper. Let's continue picking sunflowers."

Harper saw a bee and began running and screaming through her mother's garden. "What is it Harper?" asked Mom.

"A bee is on the sunflower!" said Harper who was still running and screaming frantically around the garden. "Harper, it is gone now, probably because of your screaming and running! Just be careful not to pick a sunflower with honeybees on it."

Harper was a very curious child. She just wanted to know why honeybees always sit on sunflowers.

Harper's mom saw her curious expression and said, "Bees eat pollen and nectar from flowers. The nectar is used to make honey."

"Really, mom? You mean the honey in the house is from bees?"

"Yes, Harper."

Harper looked at the flowers in her mom's garden again and began picking more sunflowers with excitement.

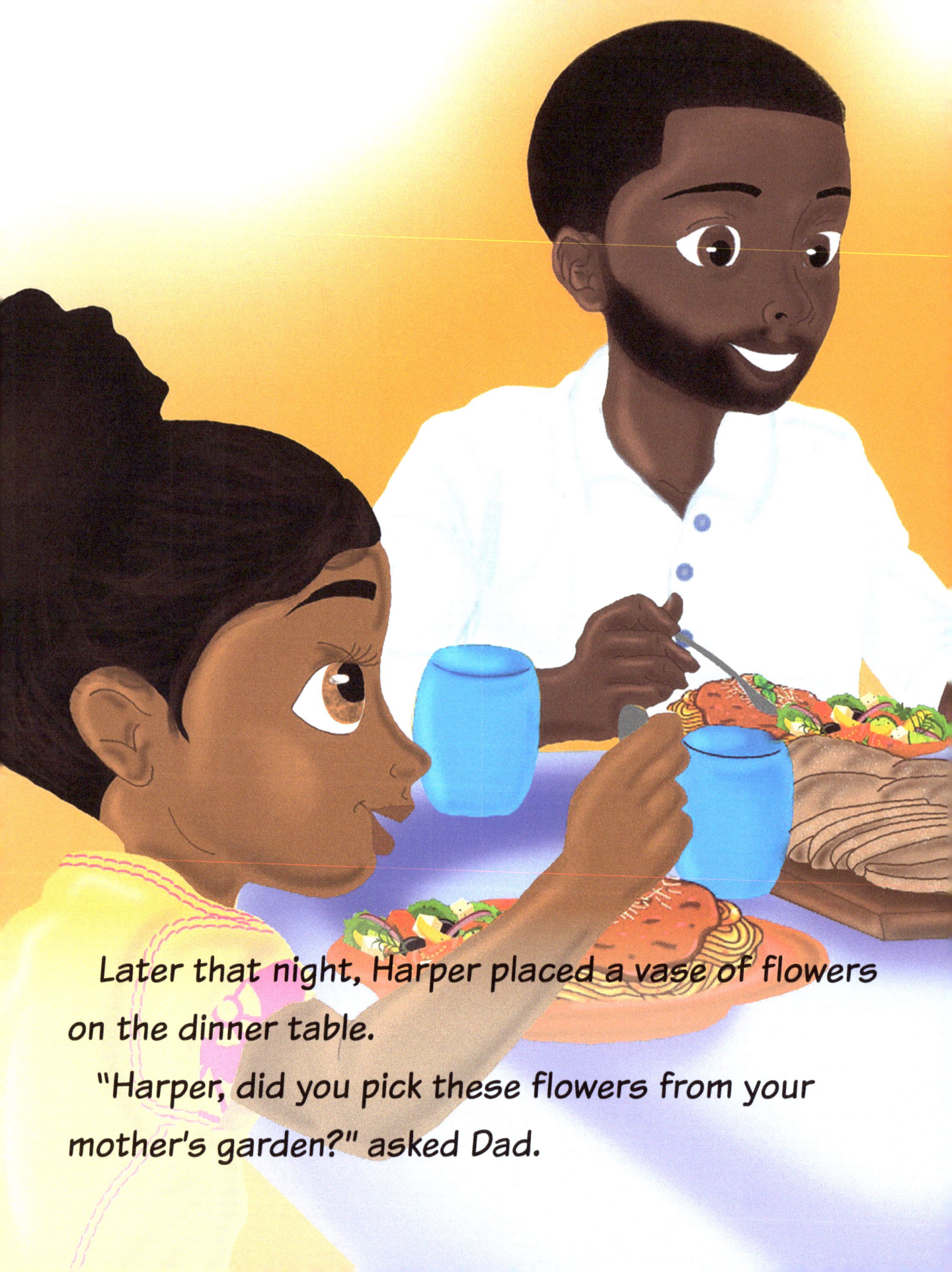

Later that night, Harper placed a vase of flowers on the dinner table.

"Harper, did you pick these flowers from your mother's garden?" asked Dad.

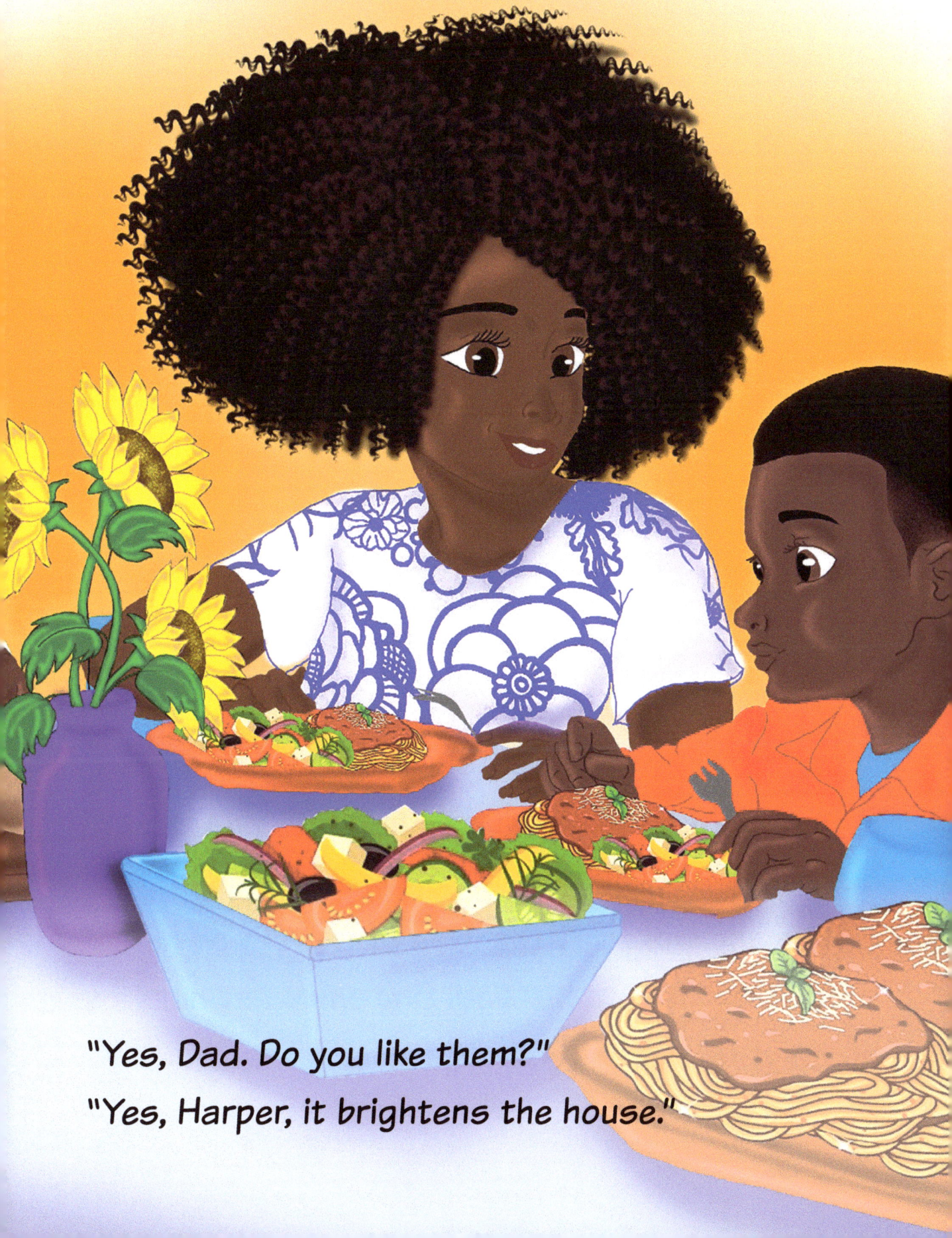

"Yes, Dad. Do you like them?"

"Yes, Harper, it brightens the house."

That night when Harper went to bed, she looked out her window at the stars and the moon.

Then she looked at the vase of flowers on her nightstand next to her bed. She smiled at her vase of beautiful sunflowers and thought that flowers were so amazing.

THE END

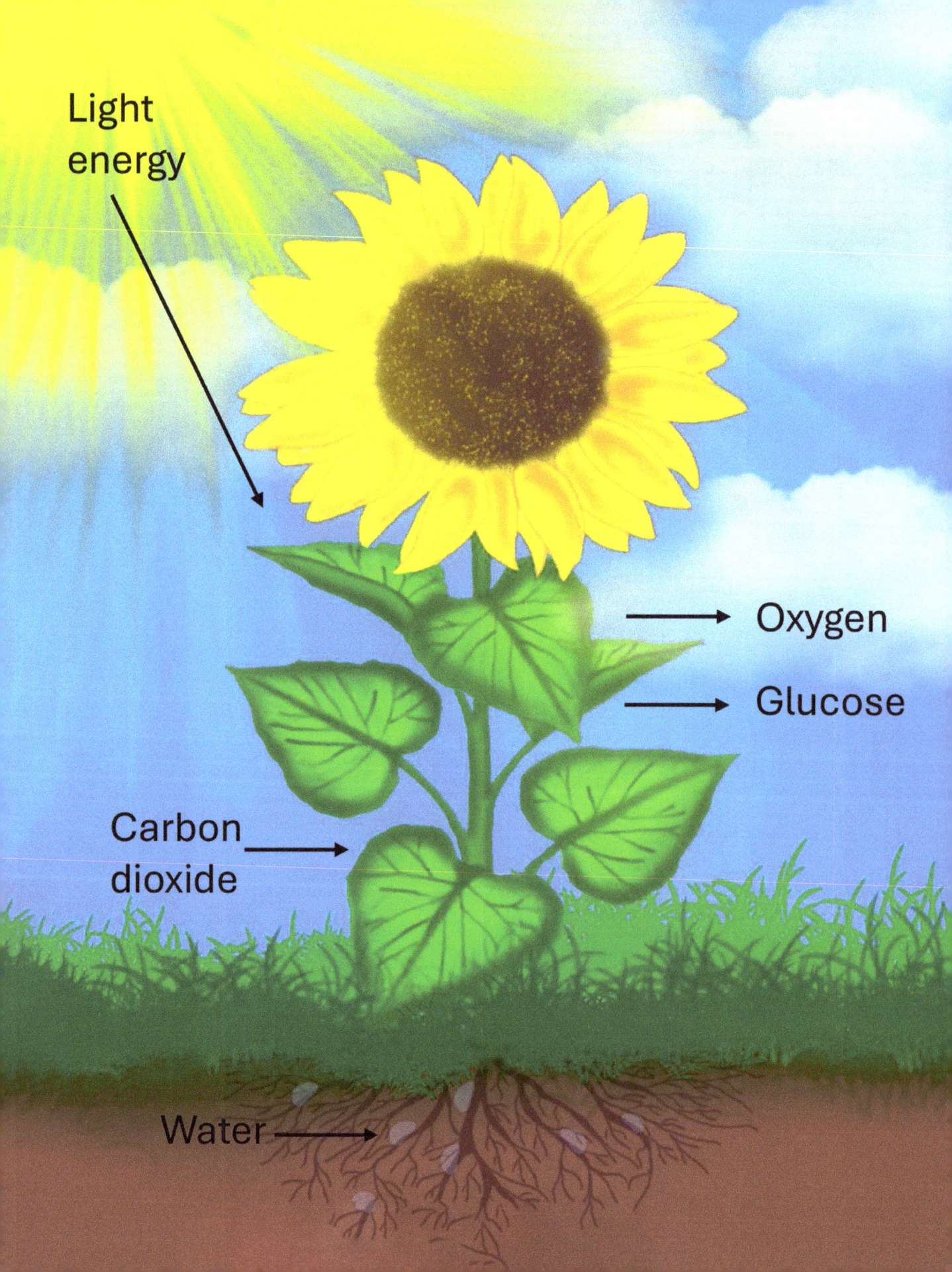

Light
energy

Oxygen

Glucose

Carbon
dioxide

Water

Knowledge Nugget

Photosynthesis is the process by which a plant uses sunlight, carbon dioxide, and water to make oxygen and glucose (sugar).

www.ingramcontent.com/pod-product-compliance
Lightning Source LLC
LaVergne TN
LVHW070840080426
835513LV00023B/2414